THE BLUE BALCONY

— Poems of Places and Times —

THE BLUE BALCONY

— Poems of Places and Times —

by Gordon King

Snow Drift Press / Washington / Maine / 1998

First Edit

ISBN 0-9661678-1-3

The title typeface is Caslon Open Face
The text typeface is Bookman Light

Cover and book design by George V. Van Deventer
Layout by David B. Martucci

Published by
Snow Drift Press
117 Fitch Road
Washington, Maine 04574
snodrift@midcoast.com

Printed and bound in the United States of America

Grateful acknowledgement is given to the editors of the following publications in which some of these poems, in earlier versions, have appeared:

Envoi Magazine
Wales, UK
Doors Magazine
Dorset, UK
Asheville Arts Journal
Asheville, NC, USA
Free Press
Rockland, ME, USA
The Island Institute
Rockland, ME, USA
The Camden Herald
Camden, ME, USA
Annual Anthology, 1996 & 1997
Live Poets Society, Liberty, ME, USA

Warm thanks are due to George Van Deventer, Arnold Perrin, Bruce Spang, Ruth Love, and to my First Reader, Josephine deBeauchamp, for their encouragement and support that helped make this book possiblc.

Cover art by Josephine deBeauchamp

Illustrations by Dan Daly

Contents

North Carolina

California

England

Maine

FORWARD

In reading the works of the author of *The Blue Balcony*, it is impossible to separate the poet from the diplomat, or the artist from the friend. In a Maine community increasingly transformed by passing celebrities and flashes of imported flamboyance, Gordon King is a breed apart.

King is a man who served his country not as a bureaucrat, but as a representative of the best of what it means to be an American; a rare combination of Midwestern intellect and heart, of curiosity of culture and language, of great generosity and humility. No wonder he loved and was loved in those Middle Eastern countries; he must have been irresistible!

These poems are a humanist's witness to the ceremony and innocence of life. Perplexed as much by Alpha Centauri as by the vision of his son as old man Moses, by the myths of the Khyber mountains as by the loss of a modest housewife killed by bandits, King is, in some ways, a closet journalist, a contemporary de Toqueville. His poetry records an inner struggle for balance between the known and the unknown, common sense and tragedy, or as he says in *A Perfect World*, the mind "entrapped in his head" and the "odd quick jerk" called the heart.

In *A Moment Lighter Than Air*, King's words capture the "casual elegant array" of the unexpected as it floats above the beautiful, in this case "the scrumbled barrens still fruit-warm and scuffed" of upland Maine. From his "box seat next to the world," these poems indeed combine the richness of the past/present with deep awe and reverence to the gifts of life, embodied in the simple swollen flesh of today's tomatoes and his loved ones.

I am increasingly grateful this fine poet strolled into our newspaper office (*The Camden Herald*, Camden, Maine) on Mechanic Street a few years ago. Typically he was focused at the moment on a local issue involving the lack of opportunities for youth in the community. Gordon has the kind of generous imagination to see life from the other's viewpoint, and imagine it not as a retiree but as the truly youthful person which he will always be at heart.

William S. Patten
Chestnut Hill, Massachusetts
April 25, 1998
Publisher/Owner
The Camden Herald, 1982-1996

THE BLUE BALCONY

— Poems of Places and Times —

dedicated to Anne King (1951-1972)

Illinois

Old Photo

Behind him: Molly and Jerry neigh in the harsh lot
next to the corn crib, Jimson weed
crowds the back corners, hogs burrow deep
in the cool dark, the pasture glares August hot

and the cows dapple in maple shade
heavy with monotonous August flies.
In front: Vernon and Earl gape with surprise
at him and the camera. The photo is made

of the water tank full from their working,
and next to it they watch from the barn lot fence,
bibbed in old overalls. Shadows are dense
and old Biff the dog is down lurking

at somebody's feet. Behind looms the white
house and the porch. Mom is there watching
the goings-on, shading her eyes, and Dad is catching
an instant of time as everything in sight

stops.

Bridge of Dreams

Once as a boy he walked from Sunnyside Farm
a mile to school, and then beyond it where
a small stream cut aslant the crooked arm
of a country road. Two bridges humped it there,

his links to the next fields where dragonflies
flew point. He felt an island, washed by seas
of corn and wheat. He thought of other skies
rippled by different winds, by clouds not these,

by clearer blue, by gentler light. He ran
down by one bridge through reeds reeling in sun
and stopped, silenced, to crouch beneath the span
and—simple as that—looked into Babylon.

And changed forever. Ziggurats were there
and Marduk's priests and soft Sumerian air.

Anna and the Feast of Christmas

She pokes her money away in cocoa tins,
bills rumpled from hungry pockets, mostly ones.
They are the witnesses. She turns her back,
wills them to quiet, rustles to some odd niche,

one squirrel mother with a weary face,
her wedding ring too loose, dressed in ecru
on green. She moves to mind the stove, waiting
for the milk gravy to boil. Its mushroom smell

bouquets the air, turns the room rich and magical.
In awe they sit, for each a Christmas orange
to gaze at, mesmerized. She touches her
chin and, monkey-like, so do they. O the warm

dove peace! The hundred smells and sounds! Their first
love learned while they were nestlings by her fire.

Cherries

An Art Appreciation

A man eyes the painting of a fruit tree:
  A brilliantly bold evocative
  treatment by a daring artist
who has moved beyond mere wood
and leaf and clumps of fruity red
  to capture essences, to force
  into the watcher's mind the soul
of cherries. Evoked to satisfy
and does not satisfy. He sits down.
  Suppressed forms, odd definitions,
  forced sublimations when he has
hungered for the illusion of feeding—

as when the cherries hung on knobby
  branches, O Grandmother—
  and you sent him scrambling up
to scruff his hide against old wood
gnarled like your old hands, patient
  and fruitful, to grasp the ripeness
  and crush the redness. A Dionysus
letting the blood of cherries stain his palm,
gorging his eager mouth, his boy's mouth
  savoring the nipples of imagined
  naiads, writhing with red life.
You sent him innocently into sin,

Grandmother, and now, hungry for fruit,
  what he wants from the painting
  are lips swollen with cherries,
sharp and pagan and savagely sweet.

Love Song of the Steady Man

He drives east from the Mississippi, the
steady man, the Interstate a wide gray belt
splitting the green corn ranks, the rows of
beans, the hog sheds humped on pastures
like slum motels. The big rigs barrel past,
sucking the air, while he passes signs: Gas,
Lodging, Camping, Food, Quad City Airport,
Decatur, Peoria, I-80 Two Miles, Slower
Traffic Keep Right. Sun glinting copper
on flat pavement, the car feinting and gliding
under him, the thought, the remembering.

For
forty miles he's been flexing the knuckle
he bruised slamming it against the
wall in the Motel where he stopped—
after you sent him away when his
hunger made him powerless. Maybe
he should growl at you for a while?
At himself?

In the midst of all this wind and motor,
he is silent, the steady man. Dusk insinuates
itself. *Will you fade like the day?* He drives
toward the world's dark, quiet in the
rushing air.

While he rubbed his bruised hand
at the Motel, a couple laughed next door.
He paid at the desk and left. The car has

purred and purred for these forty miles.
He might take the next Exit, head back
toward you, call when halfway there
(you really don't like surprises),
say he's coming, he'll do battle with
your mother, he'll throw you over
his shoulder, yes, by God, take you
across three States, wrap arms, selves,
lovely, sated, inside a different
room each night, romp in
Des Moines and Prairie du Chien,
Keokuk and Kankakee, returning home at
last to leave you pale and glowing, and
drive on.

But he's still here.
Never left. Bedded you only in
his dreams. Narrowly missed a camper in
the early dark.

Fireflies smash against
his windshield, shocked out of life.

One's smudge glows for half a minute there,
slowly white fire dying.

The Farm

Flesh out the memory of a man
with elements of creek and clan;
the grapes will ripen and spun gold
tall trees tremble, until he is told
such memories are false. No trees
can whisper where the tall corn is.

Old willows, wildflowers and wind
form Arabesques in his fertile mind.
Haunted by house and sloping hill
he traces moments back until
he sees what it must mean to be
exiled by half a century.

Where is the youngster in his blood?
What furrowed fields and narrow wood,
what maple trees and flowered fence
revive for him an eloquence?
Hard work and innocence and tears
are laminated by the years.

His earth changed almost recklessly,
his house collapsed, and stealthily
over the empty lawn, corn grew.
Although his heart knows what it knew,
yesterday in a cornfield he
saw thunderheads mass silently.

Incident at a Nursing Home

When the mother is ninety one, they come
back for a visit to the nursing home.

They have to search. She has her cards
out playing solitaire, listening to birds

beyond the dining room. They talk
for an hour while the orderlies work

around them. They know she is glad to see
them, child happy to be set free

for a spell. Then, first talk over, they move
purposefully toward the hall. They shove

mop pails aside. Next to an open door
an old man sleeps on a leaning chair,

his mouth agape. She pulls them back
and looks at him, his face gone slack,

and suddenly goes up to him
and slaps his unsuspecting arm

and cries, *Wake up! Wake up!*
You might miss something!
They hope

she tigers still, giving indignant prods
to sleeping angels and the careless gods.

Afghanistan

The Hunter
Upon falling in the Hindu Kush

Clawing at a slide of shale
toward a cliff drop to a deep valley,
grasping a gun butt, gritting his will,
sprawling on his damned belly
when he could have been rock secure,
his arms around reliable stone
if only if only he were not here
sliding, hearing his voice moan

obligato to a sure end.
Roll over, flail the stupid feet
that stumbled him here. A ten second
life for an Afghan winding sheet,
a hunter scrabbling on a slope, a cliff
below, heart hammering chest,
ears ringing, singing life as if
sharp death would spurn a guest

wet with the stench of fear.
Not a chance. Below is a manger
of depth and shadows. Everything here
screaming nothing but danger
while his mind grabs for the old
complacencies now gone, the earth
now going and his annulled
few senses about to depart.

Here then the ingredients:
the neutral sky, the peaks, the snow,
the crags, the futile gun, his tense
body sliding, the valley far below
hazy with false peace. Elastic time
shrinking to seconds. But the stock

suddenly catches. He stops. He climbs
agonizingly around while a hawk

glides imperiously over the scene.
He gouges footholds out of the shifting shale,
works his way up. He who has been
dead is alive and miraculously well
and the sky hurts his eyes, and the wind
slaps his face, and the blood
in his mouth is *ichor*. Then he stands
with the gun, and the feel of the wood

in its stock reminds him that he
mounted these cliffs for the thrill
of hunting wild sheep. A bad try.
He takes the gun and with a yell
throws it back down the slope,
and with it the urge to kill,

and he's stayed alive, and the sheep
that he hunted. And he will. And they will.

The English Doctor

A Frozen Moment in Another Place

He has a grave charm, bowing from the waist
to my pregnant wife, seeing through his drunken
good humor how taken she is. His sunken
living room is furnished in good English taste
by his Embassy, with a Chippendale-style table
loaded with more drink than seems possible

and the rest of the spacious room has a lazy
uncertain look; everything placed askew
with an elegant carelessness. We are on view
before a secret and affectionate man, busy
with bottles and glasses, watching our eyes
flickering around the room, hiding surprise.

We like each other. Isolated diplomats
making the best of things, like prisoners
exiled to the edge of a far universe
of mountains, but happy enough with our lots,
so that, on a second evening, I remember
(through bitter deep cold, shouldering late December

out with snow, bringing Siberia into Kabul)
making the trip out to the British compound
over icy roads, hearing about wolfpacks around
and two police attacked, thinking it horrible
but exciting. We look forward to friends,
dancing, talk, a party that never really ends,

goes on, warming the night toward morning,
but when we get there, shivering, his house
is open, furniture piled outside, a mouse
dead, frozen on the snow like a warning,
and inside, hilarity. We find the big room

literally a sheet of ice. A man with a broom
sweeps drunkenly at some skittering plates.
The Doctor floats softly toward us, his back
turned, and around the edges a mixed pack
of wild couples, everybody on skates.
He has flooded his living room. We laugh,
keep our coats on but kick our galoshes off,
scoop up the ready drinks. I put on skates
and one of the Soviet attaches and I keep
knocking ourselves over when we step
on one or another of the broom man's plates.
The Doctor is floating backwards, gliding
and smiling, with the other skaters dividing

carelessly to let him by. His temples are gray
and he is the one Western doctor as our need
grows urgent—I'd planted my unmindful seed
and my wife's time inexorably nears. She will say,
Oh it's impossible, our child can't be born here,
at the English Doctor's, on ice, this late in the year.

Oh it's impossible; nevertheless, it would be.
She lies on his bed, on the London Times, moaning.
Wives bring in water and towels. As if chaperoning
the Doctor sits in the doorway, looking at me,
and I am aware of blood, and a sense
of mysteries beyond my male competence

and the moans sound different, the wives
skitter busily about, their voices laughing,
and the Doctor smiles in benediction, quaffing
his drink as a blessing, our boisterous lives
increased by a one and we have a daughter born,
we, the wife, the husband, the bumbling intern.

I get some Scotch up my nose, being drunk,
and, while wife and baby sleep, I remember
smelling the sharpness of the pale December
and the stale gin spills, the tired whisky stink
even through the white dust of ice. Silver frost
makes mysteries; the windows are embossed

by its hidden artistic hand. I find my skates,
go around the room again, go in and out
of the bedroom where Warlords now plot.
The Doctor and I circle, numb expatriates
skating toward exhaustion. It is bitterly cold
and the mountains are crisp and near and incredibly old.

My wife and the baby sleep through the skaters' goodbyes,
through the knots of drunken confusion, the exultant voices,
the revelry that skating and liquor and birthing induces.
I smile at my pair, and then try not to capsize,
to skate that night as I'd never skated before,
at the English Doctor's, with furrowed ice on the floor.

We carefully speak of circumstance that night.
We skate and talk profoundly about the test
of a moment. We speak about dumb chance—a guest
at a party who speechlessly catches sight
across a room of the woman who will have
years of him, and give flesh and pain, and perhaps love.

Thus, at that frozen moment, the English Doctor,
my host, and I float over the skittering plates,
keeping fond eyes on my wife and child, while our fates
move inexorably closer to us, without succour
or mercy. While we wait to see what the morning gives,
unknowable time assembles the rest of our lives.

Afghan Love

In the Afridi manner

Where the Khyber mountains hold up the Afghan sky,
there he finds his beloved by the river bank.
By its soft green she is a gazelle,
taut and poised, eyes flashing.
She is ready to flee from him, or come to him.

He fills his mouth with tenderness,
He catches the sun in his hand to brighten his face,
He calls down a falcon from heaven to prove his strength.

He sings a great song,
an Afridi song.
He dances for his beloved an Afridi dance,
to show his bravery, to exalt his courage!

And she comes to him!
To be bride of an Afridi is to become a tigress!

Iran

To Anita Killed by the Bandits

Such improbable names: *Dadshah*, King's Gift;
Dozdab, Thieves' Water; *Pip*, near where you ended,
clad in a light summer dress. Had you offended
a man called *Ghaderdad*? Was Dadshah miffed
because you would not cry? Kevin, we know,
was killed before your eyes. So were the rest.
What were your thoughts? I judge from how you dressed,
white shoes, dark glasses, frock like a rainbow,

that nothing could have been further off than death,
nothing more improbable in your life than leaving;
only the death of birds was cause for grieving;
and then suddenly to turn a corner in your thirtieth
year, off in that God-forsaken Baluchistan,
and face the fury of bullets. What did you feel
seeing the metal tear through the United States' seal
on the door of that old workhorse of a Jeep? American

certainties were abruptly gone, terrible cries
jerked out of the dying men, the bandits came
plunging down from the rocks, shouting. You, dumb
with shock, took the sunglasses slowly off your eyes
with your left hand. Did you then remember,
fleetingly, that I had driven there first
some months earlier, told you about it in a burst
of enthusiasm? You would only tremble.

Panic was not your way. When I had told you
about the bird my driver had tried to kill,
you stopped at the kitchen door, and looked, until,
silenced, I felt the shame of it, and knew
he would not do that again. In your left hand
the sunglasses were still clutched as if the time
had come to go indoors, wash off the grime.
Instead, you were pulled along by that wild band.

Dadshah must have, in his way, been as aghast
to find his trap for gendarmes had brought these
pale-skinned *Feranghee*. His inhumanities
had been against his own. Suddenly this last
insurgency was of a different scale,
men cursing against men and Ghaderdad
louder than all the rest. Sense may have forebade
violence against the woman but fear would prevail

and at some stage, perhaps within the hour,
someone (men say Ghaderdad) turned with a gun
and shot you. Their dusky women would have run
screeching about, then come close to you to stare
at the blond hair, at the pale foreign face,
before listening to the shouting of their men...
I joined the searching parties in Kerman,
scoured the Baluchi mountains, but no trace

of you. We heard that you had left us clues
of scraps of cloth. We heard Dadshah would save
your life to sell you into Africa, a slave
to some dark chief. We heard Dadshah would use
your charms himself but that his jealous wife
sided with Ghaderdad against such cold
and foreign love. We heard Dadshah, of old,
had been a *Sardar's* bodyguard whose knife

killed his then wife and her lover. He set
off as a brigand, and when I travelled through
those months earlier—before I came to know
you and your Kevin—I very nearly met
his band, but the gendarmes were there first
and I was spared to come to you and display

my fateful zest. Above Pip on the day
the gendarmes found you, when the final worst

was known, a plane from Tehran enroute
with VIP's, I built an air strip for you—
for them—marshalling together a motley crew
of tribal kids, a ragged destitute
forgotten bunch, but we together cleared
and marked the strip, found the white stones
to form an arrow. Here were unknowns
working for an unknown. Here where you disappeared

a modest housewife, you became the star,
wheeling up in an Army truck, boarding
the little plane, all of us according
you total attention. Back at Iranshahr,
Generals saluted you, garlands of scarce flowers
softened the sky for you, we were your court
and all paid quiet tribute. The airport
held its breath. The silences were yours

until we sent you skyward with a plane's roar
and turned and went our ways. I sent a kind
colleague to collect what he could find
of yours and Kevin's things. There were far more
in Kerman at your home, all the household
to be accounted for and packed in sturdy wood
(except for the items damaged by your blood)
and shipped to Tehran and home. We were controlled,

efficient and dispassionate. Were forms
required we did them, cabled the Embassy,
counselled the local staff, did the emergency
things, wrote kudos to the gendarmes,

but eventually it ended and we made
our way back to the Consulate. Dadshah
was cornered by the gendarmerie and saw
his men and women killed, his renegade

existence ended. Sooner then because
of you. And you and yours because of me.
Well...time explains some things. This could be,
had I not met you. Death might not pause
for agents or contrivances. You wanted
peace, and it came, but in a way
you had not dreamed of. You wished to stay
with Kevin, and your desire was granted.

It is here in what you had not wished that I
remember you: your quietness stopped with sound,
your caring blasted away by a rifle round,
your fine mind trashed by an illiterate Baluchi,
your love a casualty of an ignorant hate.
I think the universe was lessened when you left.
Everywhere people, but without you we are bereft.
We should have known you better, but too late

for all such wishes. I still relive those days.
God made the funny world that it should be
left to bemused inheritors like me.
The world's forgotten, but the scene replays:
on an earth where mass killing numbs the heart,
yours was a personal, distinctive end
to someone meaningful. And now we tend
you still, those few of us who played a part.

Infidel in Isfahan

Do you remember our night beyond the quinces
when we made love, Oh *Houri*, Oh Persian Princess?
    (Daughter of the *Malekeh*
    who couldn't find a way
to make my toilet work—it comes to this
among the far descendents of Persepolis.)

With a small scissors old Hassan cut the grass,
bagged it all up and took it home for his ass
    while you ogled me with hot eyes.
    It was no great surprise
to find Hassan later at my study door
(he couldn't think what you might want me for

but it was clear to me). I felt my skin
flush like a boy's. Hassan (bewhiskered *Djinn)*
    salaamed over my two coins
    (an impulsive tribute to my loins)
while across the orchard you moved against the light,
Houri, to show your legs, to tempt my sight.

There were two of me then—the one you called,
heated with love fever, wildly ready to scald
    himself against, within your heat
    as a mad drummer with his beat—
and the other who heard the night caravan go by
and cased the moon up in the Persian sky

to see if it was full. It was and, Harlot, you
were perhaps obedient (in what you were to do)
    to that moon on the fourteenth night.
    Well—this *Feranghee* neophyte
was willing, Allah! I was the proverbial lamb
though this was no ritual, you were no Abraham.

We sat over Raki, drinking. Your Persian dress
was artfully half open. If I were to guess
    I'd say you'd given no thought
    to nationalities. You sought
an outsider, a foreign innocent like me
on which to practice promiscuity.

My dear Princess, dear *Leila*—there was *Majnun*
trying to fend off passion coming too soon.
    It was like that back then
    and I still recall exactly when
you changed, became tender, suddenly sweet
with my desperate love. You slid down to my feet

and pulled me down, and there we embraced
and somehow all happened, love without haste,
    passion on a Persian dress,
    Feranghee wedded to Princess
for one wild hour. And yet you went from there
and married a South African! I swear

at you, *Houri*, Princess, even yet. My mind
walks through the quince orchard from time to time,
    the moon is still obscenely full
    in my fantastic chronicle
and you are always ready and warm. You move,
Houri, to me in my remembered love

as if you lusted for me still. My dear,
your Boer may be some fancy financier
    but I have sent him something less
    than one untouched intact Princess.
So count your Kaffir gold. It makes my day
to think about you stuck so far away.

Pakistan

Nathia

Going up, he blared his horn at twisted bends,
shadowed chasms echoed to the engine, he
watched eagles dip, owners of the wind
that combed the heights. The terrain shouldered
him stoically. Pines appeared. He stopped
and, being an American, hungered for the feel
of the place, because it was *there* and *far* and
he wanted to make it his. By photographing
a village in adobe on an adobe slope, house
smokes looking for sky, terraces with
men ploughing behind bullocks, narrow
heights reflecting a subdued salmon light.

A mile of further twistings and abruptly
the Karakorums carved the horizon.
He stopped, got out, sat on a rock as if
to huddle below the primeval indifference
like a child under a fort of chairs,
half frightened, half enthralled.
Here again, displaced in space and time,
he half feared these sun-thrust monuments
of a race of giants, souvenirs of
another earth, ponderous, communing
less with him than with goats and God,
gaunt with age and silvered with snow,
mute and solid masses that made an
edge to a high and alien nation.

He restarted the rude engine and climbed,
the pines darkened, the chasms deepened
and suddenly he was there. The town
balanced on clifftops before him, Nathia,
an echo of the old Raj. English cottages
stairstepped behind trees up manicured
slopes, neat macadamed streets fanned

from a square with *pukka* shops, behind
which teemed a bazaar and the friendly
scents of charcoal, a medley of spices,
an *eau* of ancient urine, much used dust.
He drove on further, looking for an Inn
and, finding one, dismounted, smiled at its
Englishness while a boy in white nearby
led him to the desk, saw him through, took
him on to a high Victorian room.
Oh the Raj, what conveniences you knew,
conqueror with no questionings,
seducer of those with white skins.
He looked out where bearers brought
tea to tables around the paint-peeled
gazebo, hearty English voices relaxed
with the certainty of superiority—
but these gentle folk were Pakistanis,
practicing the past.
                                        The shadows
lengthened and the mood from sun to shade.
He walked up through the town, light-headed
with smells and sights and sounds. A tame spur
led him higher until Kotli village clung to a slope
eastward and westward Kaghan and Kalam,
those haunting names that found a niche
on maps a hundred years and more ago.
On all sides spurs and steep defiles
already deep in dusk, shadows mottled
while pine-dark arrows pricked the sky.
He watched as far thin clouds slipped
past in slow silence to reveal sunlight
a hundred mountain miles from him
capping another nameless secret peak,
and then a dozen more in slow cold

remote reality in this monstrous
private and tumbled Himalaya.

His brain flamed with the storm
of sight, the mammoth humped-up
dinosaurs of stone, the burly
shoulderers of clouds. He felt himself
the first shocked eyes in all of time
to witness such profligacy.
Like a lone swallow on the vast slopes
of Tirich Mir, he owned one moment
of an immense, detached, impassive
past. What could he ever say of this?
They will ask him, Have you been there?
And he will say, Oh yes, but it's too far,
too much off the beaten track. He would
not say, Go there. But to himself he'd say,
Go back.

Sonnet for a Dead Daughter

I see your face in a shop window, Anne,
fast gone like a flickering foyer lamp burned out,
ghosting my own. I wonder that you can
still return at such odd moments, a gadabout

who plays the star in my unsleeping sleep.
You miracle before me after long years' passing,
acting my little girl, rehearsing to keep
me father. When my best dreams are massing

you take them over, my ghostling daughter, still
vivacious, exasperated, blunt, outgoing,
bossy and tender-hearted. Such dreams will
tutor me, insistent on my knowing

that I can never think of you as gone,
with all you did, and all you left undone.

Cycle

Do you know what stopped you?

When your mother dropped you
into life, she also gave you death.

The blood she seeped you, the first breath
she measured, bordered, numbered
even while you womb slumbered.

Once out here, you practised life
unknowing, unaware, until the knife
of time struck its rude reminder
how frail is our earth binder.

Life burns its fire no matter what we do,
and we can have death stacked in a row
while single deaths scream pain.

And yet we do it all again,
we do not learn, we do it all again.

We come from time, and to time we go.

North Carolina

Numbers, Numbers

The Watcher assumes a lotus seat
on 1 small disk of air, on
1 carousel of ether, on 1 dark night,
turning, looking down,
making his mock god survey
over the 50 lights on Hogback Mountain,
the 4 on Tryon Peak,
the 100's on Godshaw Hill,
following 10 cars through town, Trade Street,
    the Highway,
1 train laboring up from Landrum,
and Earl Jones sitting at his 1 table
    swallowing 30 pills.

1 town, focus for 5,000 souls,
heads, navels, and noses,
and almost 10,000 arms
and legs and eyes
and ears. 1 Earl,
1 table, 1 room, 1 house.
Numbers, numbers.

1 hour. Earl sprawls on his floor.
No 1 is in the 1 bed in
his bedroom. 1 pair
of boots lies
in his hall.

The Watcher mourns the 1 body
through the long single darkness
until the edge of the 1 world pales.

Over the 1,000 whiskers of 3 hills
the nascent dawn up glows.
The Watcher descends to his lone house before
the solitary sun can see,
invades his only bed,
pretends sleep, and
touches 1 softly with a
    troubled hand.

The Man Who Knew Pericles
A Confession

- I -

The possibilities of two Pericles!
First, the Statesman who lifted Athens to
new heights of civilization; and Second, the
IInd, the con artist, the self-proclaimed therapist
who modelled, sang, boned up on law,
walked like Adonis, and rumpled the sack
with countless women, jock of jocks and king
of gab...

- II -

The proposition: not Pericles
but Pericles (the two of them) warring
inside me: the first with Attic etchings
in a dusty book, the other—*Hey Silver Fox,*
you gonna help me?— who knew a
sucker when he saw one. Who appealed
to some crude lingering earthiness. *Hey*
listen Man! Grab it while you can! Who
would not let me be. And was listened
to.

- III -

In the Lahore bazaar, in Peshawar's
Kissa Khaneh, on the Grand Trunk Road, over
the Khyber Pass into Afghanistan, down into
teeming Bombay, into the Hill Stations, any-
where there, Westerners have always stood
out in swarthy crowds, like pale blotches on
tanned skin...

While Pericles II debouched splendidly, count-
ing seduced women, a bed decathlon champ
who is half black and half...

...The problem is
that hot tandoori climates toughen a man
by browning the mind. Look around! All
brown! Try living, being white in brown-
skinned lands and then unable to re-blanch
the mind once returned home, so that
across the fruited plains one is bemused
by all the bickering and energy devoted
to epidermi. Tired old hate that never worked.

At three a.m., staring at a strange ceiling,
seeing an arrogant face in a stretch limo, like
dismissive certainty, seeing gross obesity
waddling down the Supermarket aisle past
seven brands of kidney beans when over there
to find one can was such a victory. The faces
lining up at checkout are mysteries whatever
skin they wear. White vs. black? Trivial.

- IV-

Letter in the POBox:
Hey Man, this Hole's the pits!
I'm telling you, you Silver Fox, these apes
are ever one a goddam fascist pig!
Last week I got myself a female guard
and thought, hey Golden Greek,
this here's your chance
for some celestial kind of woman talk!
She even had the proper shade of skin,
so Man!, I thought, a soul sister to boot!
I spoke my eloquent most charming piece!
At first she'd kid around and lead me on

right through the bars—but then another day
she saw a male pig watching her and screamed
and made as if I'd copped a goddam feel!
Far flippin' out!
My anatomical
being's in the filthy bowels of the Hole.
The executioners of bigotry
have biasly attacked my positive
existentialism. Would you believe
how much these clowns pervert by perjury?
Abuse my mail rights and my speech rights and
my elegant and legal verbiage?

Thus from Pericles II. He often writes
such jeremiads, and sometimes phones,
always collect, and eloquence empowers
his voice...
Hey, Silver Fox, would you believe
I've got my smooth black ass in a real bind!

- V -

His ass has shifted over these sad years
from Santa Barbara jail to Tehachapi
and then for half a dozen times around
the circuit of San Luis Obispo, Chino,
Folsom thrown in, and back again to Chino
and the Hole. Gutter black rounds, so ten percent
of life thus far and all for tangling with
the wrong woman. Four thousand were okay but
one more was one too much...
...At home this year
everyone waits for rain, grass rough like straw
beneath the feet. His letter crackles in my hand.
He's sent a glamour shot—red shirt, blue suit,
gold-capped tooth, a cocky, copper, glowing
gentleman, face lit up like a lamp, more energy
than Jehu...

- VI -

Mendocino. Park by a dusty side street.
Another day on a US Odyssey. Tired. Curious.
Never here before. Nice town. Next to me
a fence where sunflowers frame a yard
and stacked wood makes a little fort. I look in
on a big enclosure back of a white house,
with weathered sheds and a wire pen where fat
hens scratch for grain and chuckle patiently.
An apple tree spreads shade for some geese.
A cautious gaggle watches me and a line
of blowsy sparrows chirps obligato from
the chicken wire.

Suddenly I hear
from somewhere around front a baritone
in a Calypso tune. Got to check that out.
I stroll slowly on level with the house's face
and look at a black man, bare to the waist,
blue jeans, well-muscled frame, proud
handsome head thrown back, at ease.
I walk on past, self-conscious, then
come back, deciding I can talk to him:

It's marvelous!
How's that?
The way you sing.
That's good! You live here then?
No...North Carolina.
Ooh? Where I was born!

A door I hadn't seen
in the house beyond him opens wide
to show a woman's rear. She pulls a huge
bean bag along to where he stands. Brown haired
and smocked, she makes more trips for easel, paints,

brushes and canvas, all the while smiling
at this original, this Hercules (I have no
notion then how apt that is), this manly animal,
this stud, this bronze-skinned pet Achilles
(once again part Greek).

And now we're meeting here! (He flops
and laughs.)
That's good.
*In Mendocino—and this kindly dame
is posing me to paint!*
A model?
*Yeah! Far flippin' out! It's great
these artist types appreciate my bod!*

- VII -

Next day, more singing, and he, shirtless still,
comes strolling past my camper while I stand
taking in the morning.

You all right?
Oh yes—the painting finished?
*Not yet, Man! It's break time! Might you
have an extra joint?*
Don't smoke the things but how about a beer?
I'm Pericles!
You mean the famous Greek?
*Right on! Named for that man! My Mom was Greek,
my old man was a Carolina black!*
(We sit on the curb.) *My God, he had a
heavy hand! I ran away at twelve!
New York! Got smart real fast!
Had my first gal when I was only five!*
Come off it, Pericles.
*A fact! And four whole
thousand since!*

In Mendocino he
is thirty one. We drink a beer or three
and I hear tales of gals in discotheques,
of easy babes in bars, of chasing tail
from south to north, from west to east. He makes
it all sound simple. Not effortless—but like
a carnal carnival, something like Pan
cavorting in a field of naked buns
with no strain but to choose (there go the Greeks
again).

- VIII -

Next day another bar
and on his arm he has a well rounded
psychiatrist whose name is Maya. She
scans this bouncing rainbow of a man
with a calm irreverent eye—

Four thousand, eh?
Right on! And, Irish Witch,
with all this talent, where's my profit line?
A national treasure's what you really are.
Trade me to England for the flippin' crown!
My friend, there's no way you could get that cock
through Customs.
Hey, you get this, Silver Fox?
You hear this Irish Witch?

- IX -

I think back to
a dry retzina on Syntagma Square,
staring about me like a bacchic man
rocked by the traffic and the mercantile
explosive energies of shouting, hot,
impatient vendors, taxi drivers, cops,

and the intense dark eyes of women as they sit
abruptly at the tables in the Square
and throw lipsticked mouthfuls of sharp-edged words
against each other's faces while they sip
the heavy syrup of Athens coffee. Nights
I lunge across the restless town and sit
in one particular Plaka cafe, look up
through moonlight at the looming rock,
the citadel, the haunted mount, and wash
my kebob down with good *Fix* beer.

I read
back in my room of Pericles the First,
his "arts without extravagance," his "mind
and intellect without the sacrifice
of manliness," thus speaking for his age
and for his people.

- X -

Silver Fox! One time
this small Montana town, went in this bar,
place full of cowboys and I think, Oh Man,
good place to get your big black balls cut off!
And so I dance in struttin', singing'—Hey!
this here's your one fly in a bowl of cream!
They bust out laughin' and they sweep me up!
Far flippin' out! I never bought a drink!

Call Santa Barbara in the pre-trial days,
get the Public Defender on the phone.
He's in for rape, he says. But what's the proof,
I ask; I'm told by Pericles the girl's
a tart. The man allows as how the case
is not exactly clear.

Is it her word against his word?

They call it rape (he growls),
what can I do?

(I learn the very gal
who turned this in has charged another man
with rape but that one's been dismissed because
of 'inconclusive evidence.')
Tell me (I say) is that guy white?
Suppose he is, what difference does it make?
Well, Pericles is one-half white and fur-
thermore that half is Greek.
Oh shit (he says), another one of those—
(and cuts me off)...
My telephone
lies silenced in my hand like something rude,
impersonal. Pericles, my errant friend,
you sorry demi-Greek, you've been defined
as black. A jury in Utopia might note
that here's a white/black man whose blood contains,
or could contain, genes of those ancient Greeks,
but we see only black. Fair-minded folk
might (I suppose) note other things: the year
announcing that a Miss America
was black when anyone with half an eye
could see a fifteen-sixteenths white.
Society can do this thing.
We value ancient
Greece but even half a Pericles
can't cover up the stain of Africa.
With blood that strong our native blacks have got
it made. An unwritten rule sharply declaims
that white is always overruled by black
and from this lasting proposition and
the carnal appetites of man, we know
that we with the weaker skin are doomed
to breed (I would suppose) into a brown.
Think of the trouble saved.
Well, Pericles,
has done his best four thousand times and one,
invested one year out of every ten in jail,

to try to demonstrate that Africa
and Greece are one fantastic mingling
centered upon his loins.

- XI -

Maya and I
(over our eggs in an upstairs cafe)
discuss the Irish mess, the Middle East,
and Pericles arrives, full of his last
night's scores, but we continue talking of
Beirut—until his great exuberance
thrusts it aside...
Now listen, Pericles,
(our Maya says), you've given me a thought
of how to solve all war. We'll just create
detachable genitals—
Whoa, Man! (he cries)
Just listen to the Irish Witch!
Of course.
That way, the men can watch TV. Thcy'll send
their genitals to battle. On the field
the cohort with the longest, strongest types
will win the fight and take the whole lot home.
Hooo, Man! She's gonna send my cock to war!
Better than having it confiscated by
the Heathrow Customs. And indeed, why not!
With men like that, the future opens out—
Olympics, Exhibitions, Halls of Fame—
our greatest men could leave their treasures to
a grateful nation...
Ow! (he yells, and does
a dance around our chairs)
You Irish Witch!
You Silver Fox!

- XII -

His wild erotic life
moves in a bold dimension. Hypothesis:
it's because his mother named him Pericles.
Antithesis: it's because his skin is brown.
He calls himself "*El Golden Greek.*" He signs
his name *"Sir Pericles."*

His Counselor
writes that:

> ...he is alive, and is as well
> as one can hope for...asthma...muscle loss...
> high blood pressure...gout...he has been moved
> these several times...protective custody...
> all minor stuff...but he, this prisoner,
> is flamboyant, pushy and a braggart, all
> of which spark conflict.

At no time is he still,
that's sure. For three long years he studies law
and makes himself the jails' relentless scourge
anent the legal niceties of convict rights.
He plagues the staff, he fills the mails
with arguments and pleas, to lawyers, friends,
a Christian type, old flames, the Governor,
the ACLU, FBI, a Congressman
and me. He clogs the book with 602's
and winds up in the Hole. But recently
another letter comes.

Oh Silver Fox, I know I'm getting out!
Sweet Chariot of Freedom is upon me!
I want to go but I'm a little scared—
I been bad hurt, Man, in my body and
my mind! Out there, it's got no walls around
and I could spin right off the flippin' edge!
What will become of me?

You'll be a fire
out there, O Pericles. Don't bank your coals
and burn more slowly—there's but little time
to horse around, to sing Calypso, lay
your bod upon more bean bags. Plain to see
that you're too big for cells. You overflowed
those grimy corridors. You optimized
relentlessly. You fought for prisoners
with great determination. Golden friend,
rebellion for yourself and mates is not
the same as giving heart to Athens, but
you've got his fire together with his name.
Different worlds engender different fates.
Time is not particular in how it makes
a life. You are a man.

- XIII -

If you insist
on lust, be more selective. Stay away
from Santa Barbara (find kinder Saints).
Avoid the tart. Believe your better friends.
Get married if you can. Protect your skin.
Relax. Be well. Gain all that muscle back.

Remember me.

California

St. Francis in the City

Child, the sounds along the street
are the constant growl and stutter of a war.

It is as if the utter endlessness of noise
would defeat your senses, make your mind
forget what silence is, or trees' moan,
or what life feels like, alone.

You should not need to be in debt to city
clash or city stink, or to the obscene
plethora of goods in this urban artificial
woods. Mankind was not meant, I think,

to live like this. Sounds are too loud,
structures needlessly high, too much filth
darkening the sky, and morning gone
that was for you, Child; the freshness

I spoke of when cool pink dawn would clean
all night's dank odors, and the green
voice of the earth remembered love.

Maria, on her Tightrope Walker

Drum, though never a
scholar, is as light and
clever as a squirrel.
From morning to night
he walks along his
ropes, laughing, despite
hopes that one might
see a spectacular
fall or something
new on one of the
few times we are
all here,
a n d
w
a
i
t
i
n
g...

This Endless Night.

I toss and turn until
bed is a bad joke. A steeple clock
engorges the dark with hours. The air is as still
as a sphinx. Good time to take a walk.
Deserted streets. Head toward the beach. Row
after row of breakers coming in. A hum
and rhythmed slap of surf.
Not knowing how
to relax, forget myself, practice the dumb
waste of an hour, slip forward on an oblique
and try to pretend that here, encircling me,
lives a world without a clock.
It would be like
(foiling the usual time conspiracy)
drifting along through boundless hourless hours,
eating and sleeping and working and loving when
the impulse came. And there would be no towers
ticking my life away. And it would be a sin
to measure things. But men, the thinking beasts
who have invented time, are doomed to give
it mastery. Men are its prisoner priests
and the best they can hope for is a fugitive
myth of control.
A poem might try to aim
for a timeless earth. But even the streets are rhymed,
in parallels like words. There is no antonym
for fatal steeple clocks.
And even the surf is timed.

The Surf at Laguna

Endless drums. The power of thunder.
Gulls reluctantly up over
the heavy foam. Two surfers ride a
breaker in...wipe out.

A young blond mother with a
blond baby wears jeans so tight her sex
is advertised in blue. She climbs
the stairs, stern contented with fat,
her arms loving like Mary's, keeping out
the rest of us, the gulls,
the hammering ocean.

Ice plants crawl the bluffs below the
beach houses that primp in rows
in an eternity of good days. The surf
booms heedlessly, a bass roaring inward
from the west, the surfers like seals in the
further water, like skaters on foam,
like dancers on palm leaves in a time of
mindlessness, water and man.

A girl in red shorts and a red
band around long black hair jogs by
for a second time, and again the
beachies lounging against a near
wall snigger and laugh.

Here by the ocean it is never silent.
          Silence was left behind in
                    the beginning. The shore has
wandered, the sea has raged
          and gouged, the land has
                    surged back with deep earthen
growls. There is always change;
          nothing will ever change. Sea and
                    land, water and man,
surfers and jogging girl,
          the mother with the soft
                    protective arms,
the babe.

The Ballad of California Jack

A simple man wanders our street
and his name is Jack.
We first saw him back
where Pier and Hermosa meet.

We thought, a good lean build
like a swimmer, and bare
but for swim trunks. No hair
and no shoes. We were chilled

in our zippered jackets, but he
went on down the walk
with his elbows acock
like a sailor on liberty.

Later, we listened and knew
that his speech was mad,
his eyes vacant and sad.
Not a thing we could do.

We saw that the others were fair,
their bodies, their skin,
before the Fall, without sin,
endlessly unaware.

They knew neither bad nor good
in their fitness charade
on the seaside parade
in front of our neighborhood.

We saw many such bodies there
near the sand and the sea
where the surf brainlessly
babbles throughout the year.

Jack walked the circumference
of this transient crowd,
boisterous and loud,
dressed for impermanence,

their eyes empty and bright.
But when they saw Jack
they were taken aback
by this odd bedlamite.

He was pure in his form
with his damaged head,
fey and light-spirited,
naked and warm.

For he had no sin in his face;
he was elsewhere confined
alone with his mind
in a separate place.

England

Gull Flight in Dorset

Gulls wing in the Dorset sky,
winning sky naturally, while I
stand watching with an ache,
knowing I'm ground stuff, awake.

But dreaming—in that false time
I can leap toward Lyme Bay and mime
a gull's flight, and its grace. I fly
in magic space like Mercury.

I dare in dreams. I test my wings,
an Icarus bold with featherings—
but dawns with sunrise intervene,
and gulls wing high, and I am man.

Thoughts While Climbing the Ruins of Maiden Castle

Big as the earth it seems from within.
One can imagine
the din when skirted men from the galleys
first showed over the heights and some rode
horses with golden bits in the mouth
while the sun flashed on swords
as they slashed down the shepherds
to the south caught out with the flock,
and the sheep and the stock scattering
and the vast confusion among the *Veneti*
in their great fort built to last
for eternity.

In the winter the barren heights suffer chill
with wind whipping
the hill, but summer's long days and short nights
make the chalk paths glow white on the walk
on the crest of the piled earthen wall
where the grass grows. A look northward
shows Dorchester and the smooth
crawl of vehicles connecting the city
with wherever. What a pity we no longer
have omens: today there are only three
tourists to visualize Romans on march
from the sea.

The Blind Man

Down Broad Street the blind man gropes
slowly with dog and cane.
We hesitate and turn and stop,
made awkward by his pain.
We follow after to a Pub
where he buys a friend a beer,
joking and laughing in a club
that rocks with fun and cheer.

A bearded publican looks on
and sees our watchful eyes.
We drink and laugh and feel as one
while he pours and roars and plies
the long full bar with beer and wine,
and the tables with wines and ales.
And our blind man sipping his sloe gin
laughs at his friend's tall tales.

The blind man stands with dog and cane,
the room roars out its cheer.
He jollies himself away and then
we quaff our bitter beer.
We move to the embracing light;
we drink the other's face.
But here or out, the gathering night
holds him in its embrace.

Up Broad Street he makes his way
through lights like brilliant cones,
and we, after a humdrum day,
stand thoughtful in our bones.

Wrestling With Angels

Orion glints over Weymouth in November,
    sharp as Drake's sword slashing the night,
    harsher than the stars I remember when life
was young and in my debt for a few decades more.
Now winter comes with lights winking over
    Chesil Beach and Lyme Bay calm with
    equilibriums of water and air, sky and
sea reach, the tranquility an unexpected gift,

like a sudden sense of peace in a new and untried
    town. The shingles drift eastward with a
    hiss and hiss, on cue from a deep charge:
stars and water, the one enclosing the other, tides
obeying moon, and earth its father, the sun. Above
    me glow myriads of worlds that I can
    compare with memories of the Hunter's
Belt back when I first became aware of night,

as it seemed when I first felt the awe of the
    insignificant, wondering what was true
    in myth, certain that—even though ignorant—
I could charge up to wrestle with angels.
Where did the angels go? I see Orion over
    Portland Bill, I know its distances,
    I know how vast and strange it is, how volatile
and furious its fires. The numbers soothe, reveal;

no need to climb to stars for astral love affairs with
    some far Ashtoreth...the universe lies in my hand,
    Orion a detail. I would be, like Odysseus
home to Penelope, veteran in a familiar land.

Death of a Fisherman

The town accumulates ghosts, the
boy swept off the Cobb who
drowned because his boots filled
with water, the dozen who followed
Monmouth and were sent back here
by Jeffries to be hung and left out
in view of the town. Whose dried flesh
isolated the shore from the sea.

The town where no one can
count the dead of these close houses,
the builders, sailors, bankers, draymen,
merchants, publicans, saints and all
wives, and the couple caught by
high tide enroute to Charmouth,
all the rest, those crowded in below
the cemetery pines, the silent
assemblies. Names grown old

known only here while the world
went on. Here, some grew wise,
some wealthy, but most climbed privately
up the slopes of birth, puberty,
love, marriage, child-bearing,
death and, in the spaces, work,
repetitive, demanding, unforgiving
work. Dulled early to the sea.

At the sea's lip in this particular place,
town crouches down in its small valley,
river runs through. Of old, men wrestled
the gleaming avalanches of fish and in
the harbour the sleek ships, the high coffee
sails. No more. Now the *Beltane*,
holed, rests on blocks at the Cobb base,
another point of interest for the tourists.
Thus it is: where once a place lived by
the ancient laws, now soft distinctive
thatch, stone protective walls, the bends
of streets, the pastel colorings wait
passively for a thousand thousand stares.

The Cobb docks a few boats in a reach of calm,
light arrows the corrugating sea,
cuts the eyes, helps bring the massive
breakwater down to scale. Helicopters drone,
fracturing the town. The Lifeboat
rockets boom above the Cobb three times.

A fisherman caught by an evening squall
that swung his boat broadside when he tried to haul
one more pot aboard, hooked his foot
on a coil of line and did a dance
on the sloping deck enroute
to the churning expanse.

Shocked, he was instantly aware
through the lashed and wild dark waters everywhere
that the boat was sinking, so
that the depth was full of fish and gear
fading with him below
in his twentieth year.

A practical sailor, he grabbed a pot,
thinking to rescue it, but his most strenuous efforts got
nowhere. He came in his own time
to dark, to monotone, to cold
in the primordial slime
where the earth is old.

Thus went one sailor back to the sea,
one Englishman down to where his mates will be
lying, layer upon old layer,
so casually, so suddenly this death
done by the soft slayer
in the briny beneath.

Back in the pretty posing town
the Lifeboat returned to harbor with a body found,
the men dejected, no trace
of the boat. Tourists took one last view
over the sea's rough face,
and then withdrew.

The Old Trade

The known history of this shore begins with these:
the *ichthyosaurus* on the Museum wall
that, millions of years ago, left its imprint
here in stone, like a giant porpoise guarding
the quiet *ammonites* spiralling to extinction,
Nautili, Gryphea, Dapedium. Lives bred,
died, settled in the muck of ancient oceans.

And nearby, the gravestones of the town

settle about a Norman church. Its grey
stone walls soften with moist lichen.
It broods like an ancestor over its flock,
conscious even of me, the stranger,
at the burial I attended yesterday,
not knowing the fisherman, but to see
how the present melds into ancient earth.

Where the sun lightfoots across Lyme Bay,

out on its dazzling water go the boats,
each out to a favorite reckless stretch of sea.
They ply an old trade stubborn against learning.
Grimly they work and curse the swelling ocean.
With nets they troll the waters clean, the dead
man's mates, and turn and look back. But the church
has brooded there for centuries. And will.

Lament of a Daughter, 300 Years After, on Monmouth Beach, Lyme Regis

Monmouth could have landed here
        on this kind of day
when waves fuss like cross brats
at the quay, and the way
up to firm land is not clear,
        but clumsy with shingle and flats
of plum seaweed, and gulls cry
in a bleak unforgiving desolate sky.

        Down on this brief judgmental beach
        twelve men were hung. To whom do I
        appeal for mercy? Twelve generations reach
        forward to me. The hung men did not teach
        us. Their earth is endless silence, and their sky.

Or he might have landed with laurel
        wreathed round his head,
with his handsome hair marcelled
and perfumed sweet instead,
and a festival ready, with floral
        tributes, and shouts to uphold
his new dreams of an old crown
gained through this unconventional town.

        Jeffries hung them. They were hung. We are
        heirs to these long memories of blood.
        I wonder if it crossed his mind to spare
        even one, to turn a different calendar.
        Earth might be greener if he had.

He could have marched through Lyme
on a day like this—
people cheering at his bright
banners, and a comely miss
for a softness one last time,
while his mind seethed with excite-
ment: he would march like a king
toward castle and crown and a last reckoning.

I want to cry my sorrow for these men
and all the weeping of 300 years.
There is not room in history to contain
the tears for just these twelve. But then
the world has rarely been impressed with tears.

But it was not meant to be.
Young Monmouth's dare
brought bloody Jeffries to stand
good Lyme men on the air,
staring blind out at the sea
from whence the Duke came, to land
on a shingled beach, and brief renown,
and a bitter axe in London town.

I sometimes wish we had a world
with room for sighs, with time for crying
over the hanging of twelve men. I would hold
their faces in my hands grown bold,
and comfort them through all the steps of dying.

My Son Coming

Up the Parade I can see my son coming
in the guise of an old man. His beard
is gray, his face wrinkled. It is weird...
he pushes forward like Moses climbing
up Sinai but it is his same hair,
long, crinkled, I'd know it anywhere,
and the glasses are the same, the glare
at the world. Moses, slumming.

He's at least thirty years older than I.
He's angrier. I should leave. But instead
I must look at his shoulders, his head,
the way they will be when I am long dead
and he's filled with uneasy memory.

Could my son see me on the Parade,
my hair black and my trousers slim?
Am I there now reliving life, for him,
taking my walk, remembering things he said,
my son just passed, wondering how
to handle this moment without a row,
seeing him stopping, raising a brow,
glancing around at me, back from the dead?

He would say nothing. He would just see
some younger man with odd grasping eyes
who steps apart with a gesture of surprise.
I would stare after, powerless to advise,
and be filled with uneasy memory.

Man and Dog

For Peter and Skip

It is a staunch swimmer, this dog,
aiming, seemingly, toward France.
Ladies are exercised along the Cobb,
seeing him fading like an errant log.
They flail umbrellas, do a dance
of rage at his Master, whose stance
is elaborately casual.
                                        He knows,
this loving man, the dog has need
for water, sea, power that flows
strong salty through his legs, that does
him good. Poor dog is not a breed
one knows of, tumescent with no seed,
the early pruned.
                                        But he will pull
bold heavy on his lead, forget
all discipline when there's a gull
tauntingly out of range. The fool
did catch one once, spray flying, yet
gull and dog, startled and separate,
fled from each other.
                                        The brown eyes,
when not on mischief, are intent for
the man. The two legitimatize
themselves. Each one is the prize
awarded to the other, conspirators
against loneliness. Therefore,
we are admirers,
                                        on their terms,
cognizant of the pleasures of
their partnership. Dog confirms
man, man dog. Their concerns
define their lives: of muzzle and glove;
of paw and waiting hand; of love.

Here. Now.

The night wind attacks the windows
with volleys of rain like fine shot against
the shingled roof of my Illinois home.

It would be black and wet now, tensed
against the Channel storm if it were here
and not four thousand miles away,
crumbled into debris.

                    But time passes.
The thought of a house passes. A ghost may
lose itself in years.

                    I think, having come
this far, that what I was I have left behind,
that what I will be I can never know.

The night is turbulent. The night is blind.

The Siege

Sea go dark, dark with wind...Allen Curnow

We had storm warnings of a harsh night,
built during the day. Dark, to our right,
howling from westward past Ware cliffs
to near, as shingle piles in drifts
where the men were hung, the gale purges
our shivering windows, heavy with dirges
that moan and wail their sharp end. We are
fortressed behind a stone wall, at war
with wind. Down to our left, where shallow beach
abuts the town, thrashing breakers breach
the sea walls and explode with wild
and furious attack above a swollen tide.

The storm is primitive,
greater than human powers, incarnative
of an ultimate chaos. Its harsh breath
resolves into a reality of raw death,
of a world enormous and alive without
us, something searching the night, a brute
and strident enemy, contemptuous
of seawalls, of the huddled town, of us.

Here we are, hands cool against the two
foot thickness of the wall, nothing to do
but watch, wait, listen. Is that the door?
Can we hear something on the outside stair?
Is it the wind? The rain? The dead men
dragging across the Cobb? Will we two end
as they did, bowing before some savage storm
that makes a judge for us, teaches us dumb

fear, reluctant humility? What moves
through night and is of night? What heaves
through roiling clouds and drums the churning sea
like a great sounding board? It would be
impatient with such flimsy watchers, hidden
behind stone walls, unplanned for, and unbidden.

Ballad of The Black Dog

The village sleeps in quiet.
Only the sea seems walled.
Silently I walk the night,
mesmerized, enthralled,

keeping a hungry eye
on the savage alien stars
against the staccato sky,
the far-off posturers

where night has eaten sun,
obliterated day,
uncovered a vast unknown
in an insolent display.

I walk, trying to tune
into an endless time
behind the silent moon,
bypassing Venus's rim,

far past bloody Mars,
wondering if I can
gain wisdom from my fears,
or sense from the Stygian,

incomprehensible
and vast expanse of space,
how to regard the tribal
and vengeful human race.

I eye the secret sky,
dauntless in the night...
not often its immensity
permits as clear a sight

to put me in my place,
a path on village earth,
below the fury of space
and the galaxy's afterbirth.

I walk to a quiet light,
its infinitesimal spark
struggling through the night
against the incredible dark,

to hide from the shadowed street,
an isolated flimsy figure,
but the earth moves under my feet,
and the Black Dog grows bigger.

When the Sleeper Wakes
over Portland Bill

In the near distance, the Bill
embosses the sky,
a brontosaurus rising
from the sea, dragon-spined
stubborn   skeletal
pale   marbled   timeless   dead
spurred   crusty...

An adamant Gibraltar
petrified   perfect...

O my well-beloved
remembered on the stone
rising above the sea.

Random Street

Prospects from this flat above Marine Parade:
to fish the scene like a tourist; to see
power boats race around a course
of three buoys and return hoarse
into the cramped harbor. But I will be
above the drifting crowd; I may invade
but may not touch.
                                        The random street
holds busy faces I will never meet.

I have looked from this stone shelf self-consciously,
skimming the mottled seascape with my gaze,
watching the tourists idle along,
a mindless vaguely discontented throng,
like pigeons in the alleyways,
or actors walking, backs to me
on stage and off.
                                        The random street
holds hidden faces I will never meet.

Beyond the Cobb

South, sea glints. From this curve only sea,
flecking, turning, restless, moody, bland,
flexing its muscle against intruder man.
Surely it questions my arrogant breed
that has thrown into patient water the debris
of history, the waste, the murdered in legions.
We have exploited it as a multiplicand
of our greed. We have subverted oceans.

Man's cesspool. Sea must resent shore
with this fatal form of life on view.
We are the shape that Adam grew,
a clever mold that originated war
and invented God. Made Hell. And swore
that it would go on for infinity—
as if time too belongs to one who
came from the sea, who goes to the sea.

Beyond the Cobb open ocean will have
its breeding ground of life, and more
of which mere man is monitor.
The sea is womb, the sea is grave,
but will we listen to its grief?
It tells us old, it tells us new,
it tells us peace instead of war,
it tells us what we will not know.

Maine

The Blue Balcony

- I -

Here hangs a balcony finished in Delft blue
and boxed with marigolds and scarlet sage
and patio tomatoes and red geraniums,
topped with a feeding bowl to which a gull comes
as a winged reminder that here lies a fringe
of land and ocean. Here, a coniferous few

trees hide a harbor where, in their restlessness,
boats horn a moment already ripe with the cries
of children playing and the sighs of cars
passing on the High Street. Sails and spars,
as seen through a gap in the foliage, advertise
a world beyond this bounded teeming space,

my box seat to the world. The balcony
embraces the moment and yet remembers my past
hidden in house, buried in journal and book,
my cave, my smell. In front of me I look
over the brilliance of sage at a foreign mast
that whispers of a far and haunted sea,

and am caught on an instant. Behind me, the sum
of what made me what I am has thrust me here
into a morning multiple with life. Tomatoes grow
in rich and dusty green because I know
them well, old family friends, and boxes bear
other blooms extravagantly because growths come

as my hands remember. My past is present in me
and marigolds flower. Both house and view
conspire to meet my needs and when I am full
I am fruitful, as happy and mindless as a gull
and geraniums bloom. A balcony in blue
brings back a talent from a distant time

and I play host in a high garden to guests
who multiply. I sit and celebrate
when chickadees, like fancy sparrows, come
in their tuxedos, and finches, frolicsome
in gold and purple. Silently I wait
within the gossamer of all my pasts.

- II -

And all from a blue balcony, polychromes
in a morning candescent with sun, substantives
as primal as sex, my eyes filling the calm
with the brilliance of sage, the cryptogram
of marigolds, the slow dumb transitives
of tomatoes, the gentleness of geraniums.

The world presents me with a pantomime
of richly different scales of individual
entity, on land, on sea, in trees, in air,
each element alone and singular
and totally unique, but all of it, all
in coalescence on a cusp of time

de B '99

on a blue balcony. Though I have been
to places buried deep in years, and know
what no one else can know—why scarlet sage,
on fire beside me in this anchorage,
blows me to rapture, why marigolds
encage my eyes, and why tomatoes seem

like ripe voluptuaries, offering
their swollen flesh to me—my innocence
is a farmer's from another age and land
who touches a tiny garden with a hand,
and wonders that all of this makes sense,
man on the earth, birds on the wing.

Spring in Maine

See the smooth ripples out on the water
  painted with ever shifting designs
  sent by reflected light from the pines
and made by a teasing wind, our father

who blows from the North, reluctant for Spring
  to soft here as it hopes to be doing,
  touching the birch where grass is growing,
sending the gray doves up on the wing.

See the sky's blue, a clearer pattern
  than we've had for months. In a mortal sense
  it's the annual stirrings of innocence
on the cheeks of our grumpy Winter slattern.

Far to the South there are trees, we're told,
  that are flushed with bloom and the air is hot
  and the people have everything we have not,
but they grow old, yes, they grow old.

The Taste of Midnight

While she softs down the deep dark bed
and he sits desk-enwrapped, the wide
embracing night stills. Silvered lawns
cone-catch. Old Tom stalks over scums
of leaves. Dogs bark. Trees stir. Stars
chandelier the universe.
Behind the town, the mountains lie,
an ancient scrim against the sky.
A harbor up from mourning hosts
shadows of ships and darker masts
stirring out of somnolence
as if in April they can sense
the warmth to come. At harbor's head
a stream pours out, high-spirited
by winter's end. A windowed light
glows muted and indefinite.

A shuttered pasted store-strip street
echoes the sound of midnight feet.
A dormered manor of a house
looms silhouette and comatose.
The mapled town will sleep for hours
in innocence, while night obscures
a quiet soporific world.
This is the moment I have curled
the taste of midnight on my tongue,
throwing my thoughts down through the long
particle chamber of my mind
to split off crusted age and tend
the prospect I encounter there
in musty room and midnight hour—
that Spring will come—and I will sigh
for roses, and remember why.

Night Vision

I lie down on summernight grass
with red spruce and balsam firs
at the inner edge of the black
and stares past them at six thousand stars.
With no moon showing,
my eyes tune like an antenna
focussed on waves of night.
Steeples thrust up in
the town. The statue of a
Yankee soldier poses near
the stream into the harbor,
forever on duty.
Remnants of the old faith
cling. Town folk, country,
settlers, immigrants, all
search from time to time
like the bowl at Arecibo
for Something out there.

They feel a private hunger for
security. They wait and hope for
God. The mountains ache with
memories of God-fever as when
the preachers talked of sugared love
and evil incubus.
The long faith fingers of
the people still probe
past far Arcturus.
The town hears
the lonely clatter of a late night
semi
while the dark dances with fireflies
and galaxies.

God goes slowly, slowly to sleep
in a summer night in Maine.

Morning Walk

I start off mornings with dumbbells,
my first decision needing to be left toward
the Library, or right toward the B and B's,
and this morning it's left because I see
Cliff down the way, mounted on his power
mower in front of the handsome facade
of the building of books resting on thick grass,
its brick trimly pointed, over its shoulder
the harbor gala with boats.

Cliff stops
the mower and waves. Hey there, he says. Up
and down, up and down, that's the way. And
how are you, I say, stopping, bringing
the dumbbells to rest and smiling. We share
the sharp burst juiciness of apples plucked in
Fall, the low shuffling of cows in a barn at five
in the morning, jerking muscles awake at the
outside pump, a pancake and bacon and eggs
and sausage breakfast after two hours' work,
the albums of memory. So, farmer, Cliff says,
tough days made good men. We shake our
heads and I move on.

The harbor
spreads itself, shimmering, spiked with masts
in the early sun, and I am one two one two
around to Atlantic Avenue, skirting the
amphitheater with its echoes of weddings
and festivals, and thumping on past the
marine workshop with my mind on The Farm
and the smell of apples and pears in the
orchard, the scrabbling in the chicken

yard, Biff the dog barking, the outhouse,
seating myself over a carved wooden
hole, hoping against spiders, imagining
crawly-creepies moving onto my timid
hide.

And now a morning there moves into
my mind, a rattlesnake curled in front
of the outhouse, the mother coming with
the .22 calibre rifle and popping away at
it while we kids yelled, and the snake still
rattled, and then her coming back with the
Ivor Johnson .32 calibre revolver and
shooting at the glistening coils, holding
the gun with both hands, we kids quieted
down now with the stupendous significance
of the event, and then suddenly our father
up from shocking corn, running, with the corn
knife in his hand, shouting *What is it?*
What's going on? And all of us looking
at him and looking at the snake and he
going up to it with his knife like a big
machete, and with wicked slashing strokes
cutting the snake's head and body to pieces.

I walk too close to a tree, a dumbbell
grazes the trunk and throws me off for a
moment. Little and big shocks come that
way. A good friend's wife has just died
and her illness had hardly registered.

But I will not brace myself. One must use
oneself if only with dumbbells, being aware
of tree trunks and the suddenness of snakes.

View Past Little Island

I can see a Coast Guard ship
        hoisting up a faded red buoy,
        its bulb dripping with brown seaweed.
The ship's name is something—SPAR,
        and on its decks little orange men scurry
purposefully, working the davit
        in heaving impatient seas.
—SPAR could, I suppose, be CASPAR,
        as if one of the Wise Men
a long long way from home,
        has invested the U.S. Coast Guard
with the protection of old myth
        through an old name.
                        On the other hand
the unfeeling sea and its restless scape
        bruises the geometry of ship like a toy
        pushed by an indifference whose need
is as simple as reaching the shore.
        It makes its way with an incredible fury
of transient forms. I can no more have it,
        own it, than I can hold these
passing moments. They are too far,
        having passed. Only by my pen
might the buoy and CASPAR still come
        to life. But my memory is marred
because the waves I saw are with
        thousands the same,
                        and have reached land.

A Moment Lighter Than Air

A fall of fields, fields of blueberries
in the Fall, bleak autumnal moors
across an upland Maine, crisp and brown
on the dying hills, blueberry tills
toasted with season, with harvest gone
across the scumbled barrens still fruit-warm
and scuffed with a dry insomnia that
clings to summer; suddenly, silently
overhead, carelessly strewn through autumn sky,
in casual elegant array across the high
light-hearted air, float six balloons.

The Eagle

My canoe whispers across to the Duck Trap pond
and through to its river below the Route 1 bridge.
A breeze fingers my cheek intimately. Sound
lessens, differs.
                    I scan the rocky ledge
and dappled woods beyond for possible deer.
This is the stretch where one can see them, where
they come to drink.
                              My oar bites into clear
water. I cleave into silence, no longer aware
that a hundred yards back is the clamorous world.

I am *Aranbinau* alone and the dark forest sings
the old song about being free, and from a gnarled
and muscled oak, unexpectedly, outsprings
an eagle thrumming its broad immoderate wings.

Meditation on a Winter's Evening

The season evolves in his mind through sea and pine
into acceptance. He understands, with that said,
how he has turned aside somewhere, has had
to take more time with things, and things with him;
more time for silence and a bleached Maine house;
for gray evening and the Bay; for meticulous
islands; for gulls flying; for old enfolded snow
molding the earth like a fading bridal dress;
for oaks in charcoaled skeins; for cold through
glass, with window panes obeying the laws
of physics whereby crisp air and vapors pause
to scratch fine fleeting scrolls; for a pale sun
fringing the sky timorously, soon to be gone.

In patterns of black and white, simplicity
works on this painting, prints on his mind
the gulls crossing the rose evening to find
their niches, a woman walking by urgently,
absorbed within herself, lights winking in town,
drivers thinning on streets, each to his own
destination, the spelling out of who he is
over crackling snow, through a door, day done.
The dusk shrouds boats, an end comes to gulls'cries,
the Bay fades out. The town has swallowed night.
He turns and climbs the stairs and takes the sight
with him, a lamp, a house, a town, an Ark
of pale blue life within the enfolding dark.

A Perfect World

One night entrapped inside his head
          with high dark silhouettes of trees
                    against darker trees, and a deep maw
                    of sky above, he wondered how
          his mind knew night, and how one sees
the infinite from pillows. Spread

out before him, all of space
          began to shimmer stars. He thrust
                    his eyes into an outer dark,
                    and once more felt the odd quirk
          that made him human. But Henry just
came in, his cat, who will insist

on bringing him again to here,
          to a lap sitter, and to fur,
                    to know precisely who has come,
                    from where, for what, and with the hum
          of a benign contented purr,
he will not wander very far.

Sleep You Lovely

But sleep you lovely,
dream you easy,
smooth your hair and
still the languid
mayness after
moaning bed.

He is drunk with
singing moments
like an aching
on the tongue
when roses wax
and gardens gown.

But warm him with
a wine like woman
and, my sweeting,
above all,
do his easy
love recall

and shake a lusting
from your juices,
have your beauty
light his life...
He is bare beneath
your knife.

Upon Learning of the Death of Ada
for George C.

The telephone lies silent in my hand
still echoing your troubled voice that told
me when she went and how.
                                        I understand
how endless seasons end. I have my old
winter haunting me over the passing years,
singing often in silences, as if the snow
of a cool forgetfulness could deaden tears
and distance death.
                              I think you too will know
peace but never painlessness. The night
will hear a voice when there is none.
You will stop at the door and turn and wait
like a gentleman—
                              and remember that she's gone,
and close the door and drop your head, and try
in your vast waiting room to say goodbye.

The Old Man

For Tom O'D.

The artist found an old man whom he liked
and painted him, a big portrait
of a big face, in and a frame
with hearts carved around, and he
helped the old guy in little ways,
trips to town, or shopped for him,
or fixed the spring on the screen door,
or brought in his garden come the
fall and filled the old root
cellar. Collected mail for him. And
painted him again, this time just
standing there, older, with a piece
of firewood in a gnarled hand, looking
at it, puzzled, like—what the
hell am I doing with this?
And was a neighbor in the old Maine
way, just being there when needed
and sitting on his porch sometimes
before the weather got too cold. And
painted him again, the hair uncombed
and white as a dandelion
gone to seed, and the blue jeans
long bleached pale as Islesboro
on a misty day. And then the
man grew feeble and before some son
could get him put away in godforsaken
comfort, the artist moved into

the house with him, and painted him
again, this time the old gent
buck naked, exiting the shower,
rumpled towel in knotted hand,
looking down his crumpled chest
to wipe himself, his parts on
view and still almost obscene with
coarse vitality, still him in charge
of his needful care, but now
the man lies in a bed, too weak
to move, while the artist brings
him food and keeps him clean
and talks to him and reads and when
he sleeps, does sketches, ready to
paint him all the way to death.

The Lobsterman Lacoste

—a sestina—

His boat holds the life of Lacoste within a frame
loaded with cabin space and lobster gear,
a narrow floating world broadened by sea.
Lacoste rises in dark and has his food
and makes his way onto a dock, checks all
his warps and traps and tops the diesel tank

and throws his life onto the fickle sea,
duty, despair and habit making the frame
that defines existence. He gives his daily all
as weather lashes or ice freezes gear,
and cleans and throws the catch into a tank
to give an awakening America its food.

This makes his life, danger and work and all.
His true environment is fickle sea.
He eyes his catch in a fish market tank
and looks at those on land caught in a frame
of solid earthy things, but sleep and food
and endless tinkering with savaged gear

make of the land a kind of prisoner's tank
in which he thrashes, anxious to leave it all,
find freedom in his hunt for the dark food
within the liquid jungle of the sea,
treating his boat as God's—or the Devil's—gear
and one with himself as with a lover's frame.

Farmer of oceans, seeker of salty food,
caught in his own immense aquarium tank,
cursing his fate, fondling his trusted gear,
certain there will be bitter days and all,
but certain too of his worth and his frame
house and wife and kids. His mistress sea

slaps the planks of the boat, and his gear
groans, and he curses the filthy food
he hauls from below and the heavy frame
of the trap, but he knows that the tank
brims with lobster, and he knows that the sea
is the fruitful beginning and end of it all.

Lacoste has it all: a watery hell called sea,
a heaven called food, loaded into a frame
called boat, filling a tank, his hands the gear.

Reflections on Global Warming

Ranks of scientists have said
Spring moves slowly to the north.
Earth portrays what it portends:
brown cones on the evergreens
        where trees are dying.
Our near is no longer near.
We shall have to move our dead.
        Is the sky no longer clear?
Are our infamies on earth
        intensifying?

We shall migrate with the trees.
We shall paint the maples red.
You will move along with me,
roses in our hands, and see
        what world awaits us.
We shall take flight from the sun
to a new antipodes.
        Tides rise up toward house and home,
and nothing, nothing they have said
        exonerates us.

We will move north, I propose.
Solid science is afraid
that we really should prepare
for some milder northern air
        somehow to save us.
If we listen will we know
where a better garden grows?

Does it follow, when we go,
that the errors we have made
will not enslave us?

Lover, is the house too small?
Will we fill it with our wreck?
We must turn our lamps to low,
carry with us what we know,
and little more.
(We must live with ice and space,
virgin and alluvial,
in an uncorrupted place,
we destructively unique
homo superior.)
We are packing. You shall be
comfort as we try to screen
the malevolence of fears,
sorting out our better years
and timeless sorrows.
We shall struggle to disprove
intelligence is deadly.
O come with me and be my love...
we shall be absolved of sin,
until tomorrow's.

Loft Poem

In his cabin in the ocean air
photographs cover a mirror,
        paintings the panelled walls;
a tinted, tilted globe of Earth
        tells him where he is;
a National Geographic Universe
        makes an ultimate tour brochure;
a Kashan carpet crowds with memories;
shelves after shelves hold books, old friends;
a CD player obeys his probing finger
and Mozart permeates the room.

An exercycle sulks like a stolid coach
        charged with maintaining him,
but he broods about his cubicle
        dressed in his casual sweats,
an athlete of the mind, riding his swivel chair,
stroking the keys that speak his language,
scanning the screen to see what he has said,
        orator to a gathering of his selves.

Wanting to find love in a coffee mug;
a figure thrown into the air by ghosts
        tumbling on an uncertain tousled bed.

Oh yes. The Earth. Sunday. America.
Wherever. Whenever.

Like a migrating Monarch,
he has been trying to get to the end
of the world, and he has almost made it.

Toward the Constellation Orion

Look at him. His name is Adam.
Like the first flushed apples on the tree,
he has multiplied, he has been fruitful.
He is his ancestor from olden times;
he is his own breeder, and his son's son,
and he has grafted for tomorrow
when the pickers come, and again
comb bright stars through the branches.

But today is the day of juices,
the day of his ripe fruit falling,
the day to remember the Book
that spun its magnificent tale
of him before he knew evil.

In the great Garden he was made,
he has been told, in the image of God.
On this earth, like a chosen jewel,
with its Greater Light that rules the day
and its Lesser Light that rules the night,
the one God made him in His image
here at the center of things.

Made Adam in His image and gave him
dominion over fish, fowl, and over every
living thing here on this jewel of a world.

But Adam has fornicated with the nights
and the revolving days, fled from
the Garden into every raucous niche,
grotesquely grown to straddle oceans,
leaped over the noisy land, split the broad

seas, cleaved the turbulent air, and now,
beyond, moved into the realm of Heaven
from here at the center of things.

The Universe hovers above his eyes
from the jeweled earth. There glow the
Greater Light, the Lesser, like lanterns
burning in his brain. Beyond them
(He made the stars also), Andromeda,
the nebulae, Sagittarius, the Magellanic
clouds, the planets. And somewhere
there, the pebble Adam has thrown
away from the fair earth, where he has
dominion over all, here at the center of things.

His pebble, flung at furious speeds
through the nothingness beyond air,
took years to leave his local borders
in space, and it will be eons from now,
after blackness and far star-pricked
total skies, before this small stone
will near the closest neighbor of
the Greater Light, with all of the
Milky Way, and the rest of the
Universe, still ahead.

By then the apple tree will be gone,
thousands of generations will be gone.
His fruit will have been
dust for a hundred thousand years
here at the center of things.

Beyond Alpha Centauri his pebble
will crawl across the vast,
ticking off the millenia like minutes.
When the Garden will be beyond
archeology, beyond anthropology
here at the center of things,
his stone will be
one short span further, across
one small arc, on
one radius, of this
one galaxy.

Ah, Adam! Ah, pebble!
His bones etched like the first fossil's
will be gone, his jewelled Earth will be gone,
the Greater and the Lesser Lights
will shine no longer when his missile
coasts through other nearby galaxies,
early early on its lonely course,
and floats on toward billions more.
He ate the first apple from the tree.
He picked the last apple from the ground.
He nourished the roots, and the branches
gnarled with time. It is the first day.
It is the last day. He is the first man
and the last, and his next step
moves him further from the Garden.